Monkey & Elephant's Worst Fight Ever!

Michael Townsend

Alfred A. Knopf

One evening, Monkey set out to bring his best friend, Elephant, a surprise gift....

But before he could knock on the door, he saw something shocking.

Why . . . why wasn't I invited to the costume party? I **LOVE** costumes!

Feeling confused, and a little bit tearful, Monkey ran off into the jungle.

THUMP THUMP THUMP THUMP

And paint beautiful faces on them!

And we always watch pro wrestling together. I don't get it.

Monkey quickly went from feeling sad . . .

. . . to feeling mad.

Monkey decided to get even.

The next morning, Elephant was shocked when he discovered what Monkey had done.

Why . . . why would Monkey do this? We're best friends. We do everything together.

He helps me collect smells for my smell collection!

Then Elephant got mad too.

He decided to get even by giving the Bunny family the keys to Monkey's house.

Monkey retaliated by painting a face on Elephant as he took a nap.

Of course, things didn't end there.
They only got worse.

Eventually, an all out war developed.

Nobody knew exactly what had happened, but they did know the Island was becoming a very un-safe place.

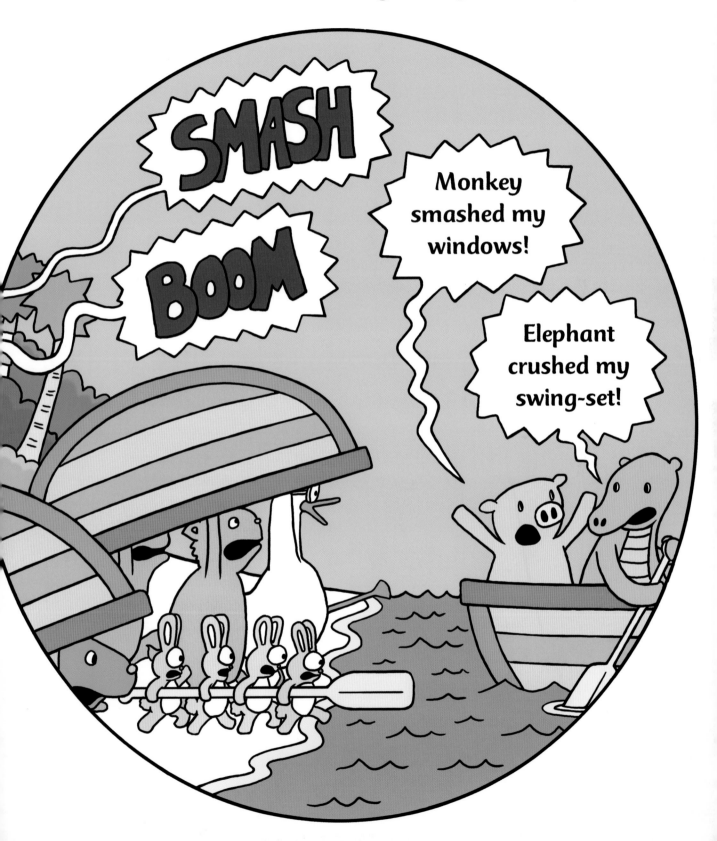

Something had to be done. Many ideas were put forth, but none were very good.

Eventually, Professor Duck came up with a great one! Massive planning ensued.

Later that night, Operation: Sink or Swim was launched.

The next morning, Monkey and Elephant woke to a big surprise.

Elephant, who was an excellent swimmer, was all set to swim back when . . .

Monkey, who could not swim, found a gift with his name on it.

It was not a Jet Ski.

Monkey had no need for a hammer and chisel,
but he did not want to share his gift with Elephant.

Monkey was *sooo* embarrassed!

Elephant felt bad too.

When the apologies and hugs ended, Monkey and Elephant worked together and made their way home.

Everyone was happy to see them return.

They were even happier after Monkey and Elephant fixed everything they had broken.

Later that night, the "not so surprise" wrestling tournament took place!

Monkey and Elephant made the best team ever!

Finally, things were back to normal on the tiny island.

Well . . . almost back to normal.

THE END